Where Are You Now?

Tyler Clark Burke

Owlkids Books

Owlkids Books acknowledges the financial support of the Canada Council for the Arts,
the Ontario Arts Council, the Government of Canada through the Canada Book Fund (CBF) and the
Government of Ontario through the Ontario Creates Book Initiative for our publishing activities.

Published in Canada by   Published in the US by
Owlkids Books Inc.   Owlkids Books Inc.
1 Eglinton Avenue East   1700 Fourth Street
Toronto, ON M4P 3A1   Berkeley, CA 94710

Library of Congress Control Number: 2018963958

Library and Archives Canada Cataloguing in Publication

Burke, Tyler Clark, author, illustrator
Where are you now? / Tyler Clark Burke.

ISBN 978-1-77147-367-5 (hardcover)

I. Title.

PS8603.U73765W54 2019   jC813'.6   C2018-906589-3

Edited by Karen Li | Designed by Tyler Clark Burke

Manufactured in Shenzhen, Guangdong, China, in April 2019, by C & C Offset
Job #HT1733

A   B   C   D   E   F

Publisher of Chirp, Chickadee and OWL
www.owlkidsbooks.com

Owlkids Books is a division of bayard canada

For loved ones,
near and far

Where are you now, star?
You danced through the sky,
As quickly you vanished,
Now where is your light?

I see you now, star—
In the twinkling sand,
In the rocks and sea glass,
Your dust in the air.

Where have you gone, snowflake?
So slowly you fell,
Unfolding to water,
In the cup of my hand.

I see you now, snowflake—

In the fog and the mist,

Swirling up to the clouds,

Rolling down to the hills.

Where are you now, seed?
Buried deep in the earth,
Can you hear us above,
As we kneel on the ground?

I see you now, seed—
In the strength of your bark,
Your branches like arms,
My cradle, your trunk.

Where have you gone, apple?
And the flower before you…
Your bright, heavy shape,
Whittled down to a core.

I see you now, apple—
In the harvest each fall,
My blood is deep red,
My shadow is long.

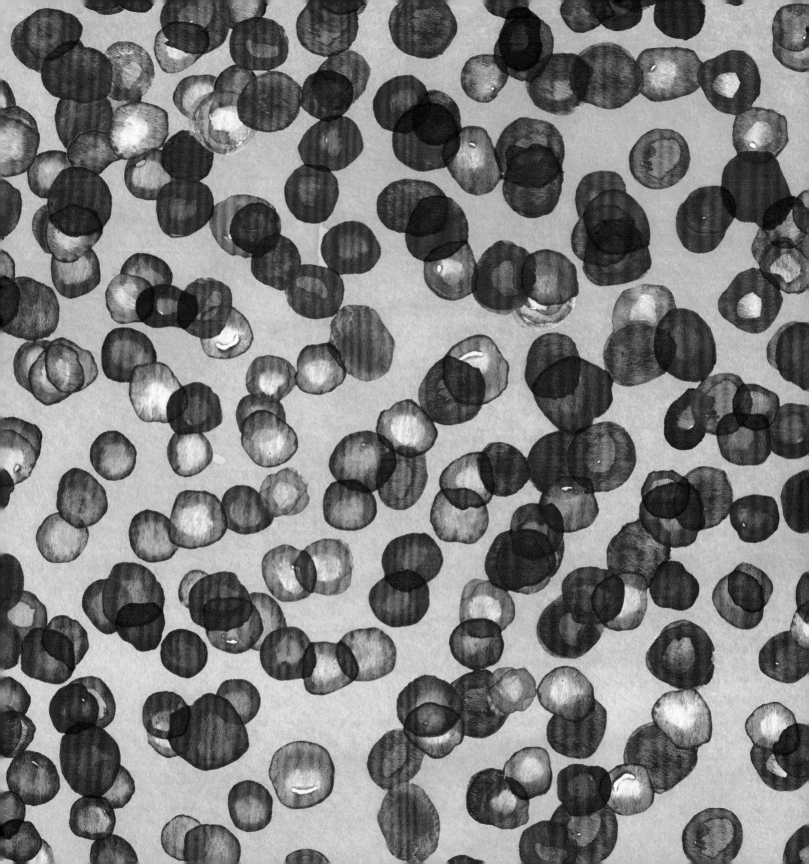

Where are you now, child?
When your eyes were just mine,
Our dreams intertwined,
Slow days, quickly past.

I see you now, child—
In your child too,
Little smile, a crescent,
A sliver of moon.

Where have you gone, now?

You were rock, I am sand,

In your footsteps I tread,

In your shadow I long.

I see you now, still—
Even though you aren't here,
Your voice and your laughter,
Echo brightly to me.

Where are you now, sun?
As the sky has just drawn,
A blanket of stars,
From evening till dawn.

I see you now, sun—
The moon casts your light,
In the darkest of hours,
You shimmer through night.

For my mother,
Valerie Clark Burke

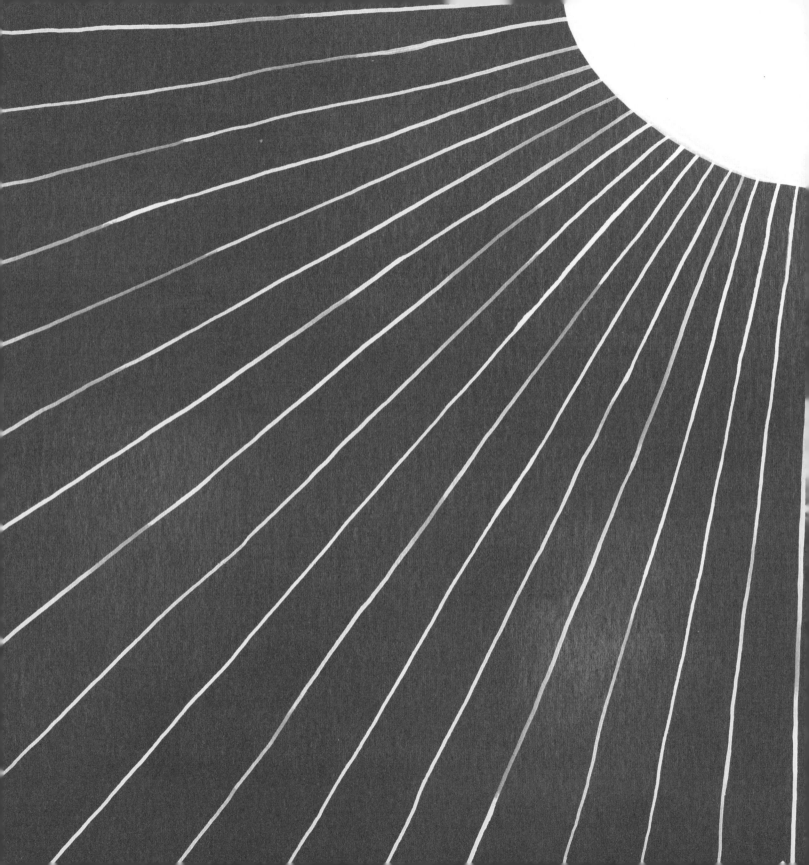